This
Treasure Cove Story
belongs to

POPPY'S PARTY

A CENTUM BOOK 978-1-912841-40-0
Published in Great Britain by Centum Books Ltd.
This edition published 2019.

1 3 5 7 9 10 8 6 4 2

Centum Books Ltd, 20 Devon Square, Newton Abbot,
Devon, TQ12 2HR, UK.

www.centumbooksltd.co.uk | books@centumbooksltd.co.uk
CENTUM BOOKS Limited Reg. No. 07641486.

A CIP catalogue record for this book is available
from the British Library.

Printed in China.

centum

A Treasure Cove Story

DreamWorks TROLLS

POPPY'S PARTY

by Frank Berrios

illustrated by Fabio Laguna,

Gabriella Matta and Francesco Legramandi

This is Troll Village.
It is the happiest place
– with the happiest trees
and the happiest creatures.
They are called Trolls.
It is also the place
Poppy calls home!

Poppy loves
to dance and sing.
She also loves to sing
and dance. And today
she gets to do both!
She is very excited.

Poppy is going to throw
the biggest, loudest,
craziest party ever!
King Peppy can't wait!

Everyone is getting
ready for Poppy's party.
But first Poppy has to
hand out the invitations!

Poppy's friend Smidge
is super small but super strong.
She gives Poppy a super lift!

Poppy brings
Biggie an invitation.
He is a big softie.
He cries happy tears.

Poppy visits Creek.
He always gives good
advice and everyone
hangs on his every word.
Creek is a super-cool Troll.

oppy knows that Guy Diamond
will make her party shine. He shakes
off a cloud of glitter whenever
he dances!

Poppy drops in to see the twins, Satin and Chenille.

Poppy's fashionable friends
will create awesome dresses
for her to wear before, during
and after the party!

Poppy practises her dance moves
with Cooper. No one can dance
like Cooper. That's because he
is the only Troll with four feet!

DJ Suki is creating a special
playlist for Poppy's after-party.
DJ Suki uses all sorts of
critters to make music.
She is always ready
to drop the beat!

Poppy's friend Fuzzbert loves to tickle the Trolls. He is also a tickler on the dance floor!

Branch
is a very
different
Troll.

He does not like
to sing. He does
not like to dance.
He does not like to
sing or dance or hug!

Poppy gives Branch
a special invitation.
She knows she can help
him find his true colours.
With a song in your heart,
you can do anything!

At the party, Smidge sends glitter sparkles into the sky. DJ Suki turns up the volume. She makes it loud!

The Trolls sing and dance, and hug and sing and dance and hug at Poppy's biggest, loudest, craziest party ever!

Everything is rainbows
and cupcakes.
Hug Time!